AuthorHouse™
1663 Liberty Drive
Bloomington, IN 47403
www.authorhouse.com
Phone: 1 (800) 839-8640

Published by AuthorHouse 06/10/2019

ISBN: 978-1-7283-1526-3 (sc)
ISBN: 978-1-7283-1525-6 (e)
.

Print information available on the last page.

authorHOUSE®

In the City, was inspired by a song that Dr. Yawza! sang to his youngest daughter during a trip to New Orleans for Essence Music Festival. It was early morning, and she had just woken up and was looking for her momma. From the view from the hotel room they could look out and see and hear the hustle and bustle of the city. Surprisingly, his daughter loved the song and thus *In the City* was born.

LOOK AT THE CITY
SEE THE SHIPS SAIL BY
SEE THE WIND FILL THE SAILS
WAVE TO THE SAILORS AS THE SHIP SAILS BY
RIGHT IN FRONT OF YOUR EYES

Share your Experiences

Share your Experiences

About the Author

New York City native, Dr. Nana Yaw Adu Sarkodie, is a Family Physician in Baltimore, Maryland. As a husband and a father, his professional and personal lives have connected in ways he never imagined. *In The City* is his first children's book inspired from the wonders of raising his two daughters. Dr. Yawza!, as he is affectionately known as to his family and friends is an avid reader and collector of comic books, a foodie, and enjoys spending time with his family. He holds a Masters in Public Health from Columbia University, and a medical degree from Ross University School of Medicine. *In The City* is the first of a series of children's books from Dr. Yawza! that will take children on a literary journey of new experiences. Dr. Adu-Sarkodie is also a member of Kappa Alpha Psi Fraternity, Incorporated.

About the Illustrator

Terrell Lamont Bunch, Sr. is a high school Visual Arts teacher in New York City. As a Visual Arts educator he has been able to connect with students through the realm of art and expression for over 10 years. His work has been displayed at Eagle Academy at Ocean Hill in Brooklyn, he has partnered with the Eagle Foundation, a non profit organization on a mural project that recreated images of African American icons such as Shirley Chisolm and James Baldwin, and has proudly contributed to his alma mater with a school logo design at the historic Boys and Girls High School in Brooklyn, New York. Mr. Bunch holds degrees from Virginia State University in Fine Arts, and a Masters in Art Education & Early Childhood Development from CUNY Brooklyn College. Terrell believes that children learn best when provided with creative learning opportunities to build a sense of self. Mr. Bunch is also a member of Kappa Alpha Psi Fraternity, Incorporated.